Four Friends in the Garden

Sue Heap

WALKER BOOKS
AND SUBSIDIARIES

LONDON · BOSTON · SYDNEY · AUCKLAND

One sunny day
the four friends
are in the garden.

Florentina the bear is gently swinging.
Rachel the rabbit is nibbling clover.
Mary Clare is making daisy-chains.
Seymour the sheep is sitting on his hill.

"Ooof!" says
Florentina.
"I am hot."
She kicks off
her slippers.

A butterfly lands
on her foot.
"Aaah!" she sighs.
"How beautiful!"

"Rachel, Seymour, Mary Clare," calls Florentina.
"Look! A butterfly has landed on me!"
She waits with her foot in the air.
The butterfly shivers its wings ...

and flies away.

"What butterfly?" asks Seymour.
"Where?" asks Rachel.
"Was it on your foot?" asks Mary Clare.

"There it goes!" calls Florentina, and she gets up and runs towards the lemon tree.
The others come running after her.

"There it goes!" calls Florentina,
and she runs towards the rose bushes.
The others come running after her.

"There it goes!" calls Florentina again.
But Seymour is hot and cross.
"There is no butterfly," he says, stopping.

"I can't see it," says Rachel.
"Why does it keep going away?"
asks Mary Clare.

Seymour goes back to sit on his hill.
Mary Clare and Rachel go too.
For a moment they're all quiet together.

Then the butterfly lands on Seymour's hand.
"Aaah!" they all say. "How beautiful!"
The butterfly shivers its wings …

and flies away.

Seymour, Rachel and Mary Clare run round and round the garden.

"There it goes!" they shout.

"There it goes!"

"There it goes!"

"There goes the butterfly!"

But now,
where is the butterfly ...
and where is Florentina?

"Here are her slippers," says Rachel.
"She's gone," says Mary Clare.
"Like the butterfly," says Seymour.

And then they hear ...

"Yoo-hoo! Lemonade!"

and Florentina is back,
carrying a tray with
a jug and four cups.

They sit in the grass and
drink iced lemonade together.
"Four friends in the garden," says Seymour,
"one, two, three, four."
Just then the butterfly lands on Florentina's nose.
"Five," whispers Florentina.
"What a lovely day!"